LITTLE HOUSE
Laura Ingalls Wilder

MY FIRST LITTLE HOUSE BOOKS

WINTER DAYS
⤳ IN THE ⤳
BIG WOODS

ADAPTED FROM THE LITTLE HOUSE BOOKS

By Laura Ingalls Wilder

Illustrated by Renée Graef

HARPERCOLLINS PUBLISHERS

For Tim
—R.G.

Winter Days in the Big Woods   Text adapted from Little House in the Big Woods, copyright 1932, 1960 Little House Heritage Trust.
Illustrations copyright © 1994 by Renée Graef   Manufactured in China. All rights reserved.   Library of Congress Cataloging-in-Publication Data
Wilder, Laura Ingalls, 1867–1957.   Winter Days in the Big Woods / adapted from the Little house books by Laura Ingalls Wilder ; illustrated by
Renée Graef.   p.   cm. — (My First Little House books)   Summary: A young pioneer girl and her family spend the winter in their log cabin in
the Big Woods of Wisconsin.   ISBN 0-06-443373-0 (pbk.)   [1. Frontier and pioneer life—Wisconsin—Fiction.   2. Family life—Wisconsin—
Fiction.   3. Wisconsin—Fiction.]   I. Graef, Renée, ill.   II. Title.   III. Series.   PZ7.W6461WI 1994   [E]—dc20   93-45883   CIP   AC
Typography by Christine Kettner   ❖   HarperCollins®, 📖®, and Little House® are trademarks of HarperCollins Publishers Inc.
Visit us on the World Wide Web! www.littlehousebooks.com

Illustrations for the My First Little House Books are inspired by the work of Garth Williams with his permission, which we gratefully acknowledge.

Once upon a time, a little girl named Laura
lived in the Big Woods of Wisconsin in a little
house made of logs.

and Baby Carrie were comfortable and happy in their little house in the Big Woods.

Outside it was cold and snowy, but the little log cabin was snug and cozy. Pa, Ma, Laura, Mary,

Other times Pa would tell stories. When Laura
and Mary begged him for a story, he would take
them on his knees and tickle their faces with his
long whiskers until they laughed out loud. His
eyes were blue and merry.

Sometimes Pa would take down his fiddle and sing. Pa would keep time with his foot. Laura and Mary would clap their hands to the music when he sang:

"Yankee Doodle went to town,
He wore his striped trousies,
He swore he couldn't see the town,
There was so many houses."

But the best time of all was at night, when Pa came home. He would throw off his fur cap and coat and mittens and call, "Where's my little half-pint of sweet cider half drunk up?" That was Laura, because she was so small.

After the day's work was done, Ma would sometimes cut out paper dolls for Laura and Mary. She drew their faces on with a pencil, and cut dresses, hats, and ribbons out of colored paper so that Mary and Laura could dress their dolls beautifully.

into a little loaf. Ma even gave them a bit of
cookie dough to make little cookies.

On Saturdays, when Ma made the bread, Laura
and Mary each had a little piece of dough to make

Laura liked the churning and baking days best of all. Ma had to churn the cream for a long time until it turned into butter. Mary could sometimes churn while Ma rested, but Laura was too little.

In the mornings Laura and Mary helped Ma wash the dishes and make the beds. After this was done, Ma began the work that belonged to that day. Each day had its own proper work. Ma would say:

"Wash on Monday,
Iron on Tuesday,
Mend on Wednesday,
Churn on Thursday,
Clean on Friday,
Bake on Saturday,
Rest on Sunday."

Soon the first snow came, and it was very cold. In the mornings the windows were covered with beautiful frost pictures of trees and flowers and fairies. Ma said that Jack Frost came in the night and made the pictures while everyone was asleep. Laura and Mary were allowed to use Ma's thimble to make pretty patterns of circles in the frost.

By the time winter came, the little house was full of good things to eat. Laura and Mary thought the attic was a lovely place to play. They played house by using the round orange pumpkins as tables and chairs, and everything was snug and cozy.

Ma, Laura, and Mary gathered potatoes and carrots, beets and turnips, cabbages and onions, and peppers and pumpkins from the garden next to the little house.

Winter was coming to the Big Woods. Soon the little house would be covered with snow. Pa went hunting every day so that they would have meat during the long, cold winter.

Laura lived in the little house with her Pa, her Ma, her big sister Mary, her baby sister Carrie, and their good old bulldog Jack.